HOW TO ASSEMBLE THE MOBILE

To assemble the Christmas mobile, first slot together the two circular pieces, taking care to match up the scenes.

Then, take some strong thread, such as button thread, clear nylon thread or fishing line. Cut a piece about 1m (3 ft) long, and tie it firmly to the ready-made hole at the top of the circular pieces.

Next, feed the thread through the two holes in the star, leaving a gap of at least 10cm (4 inches) between the star and the circle.

Finally, find somewhere to hang the mobile.

USBORNE BIBLE TALES

THE CHRISTMAS STORY

Retold by Heather Amery

Designed by Maria Wheatley
Illustrated by Norman Young

Language consultant: Betty Root
Series editor: Jenny Tyler

This is Mary and Joseph.

They lived a long time ago in Nazareth. Joseph was a carpenter. Mary was expecting a baby soon.

They went to Bethlehem.

Mary and Joseph had to walk most of the way.
They had to register to pay their taxes.

Bethlehem was full of people.

Mary and Joseph tried to find a room to sleep in.
But everywhere was already full.

They stopped at the last inn.

"All my rooms are full," said the innkeeper, "but you can sleep in the stable, if you like."

The stable was warm and clean.

Joseph made a bed of straw for Mary. He covered it with his cloak. Mary lay down. She was very tired.

That night her baby son
was born.

Mary called him Jesus. She put him in clean
clothes and made a bed for him in a manger.

Near the town were some shepherds.

They slept near their sheep to guard them from wild animals. It was very quiet and dark that night.

Suddenly, there was
a bright light.

The night sky was filled with light. The shepherds
woke up with a start. They were very scared.

An angel spoke to them.

"Don't be afraid. Go to Bethlehem. In a stable, you will find a baby who is Christ the Lord."

The shepherds went to Bethlehem.

They soon found the stable and knelt in front of the baby. They told Mary what the angel had said.

The shepherds were very happy.

They told everyone in Bethlehem about Jesus.
Then they went back to their sheep, singing to God.

Far away were three Wise Men.

They saw a very bright star moving across the sky.
It meant something special had happened.

They followed the star.

After many days, it stopped over Bethlehem. The Wise Men knew they had come to the right place.

The Wise Men found Jesus.

They went in and saw Mary with her baby. They
knelt down and gave the presents they had brought.

Mary and Joseph went home.

They took baby Jesus on a very long, hard journey.
At last, they were back home in Nazareth.

First published in 1997 by Usborne Publishing Ltd, 83-85 Saffron Hill, London EC1N 8RT, England. Copyright © 1997 Usborne Publishing Ltd.
The name Usborne and the device ☺ are Trade Marks of Usborne Publishing Ltd. All rights reserved. No part of this publication may be reproduced, stored in a retrieval system, or transmitted in any form or by any means, electronic, mechanical, photocopying, recording or otherwise, without the prior permission of the publisher. UE First published in America in August 1997. Printed in Belgium.

NOTES FOR PARENTS

The Christmas Story has been specially written in such a way that young children can succeed in their first attempts to read.

To help achieve this success, first read the whole story aloud to your child and talk about the pictures. Then encourage your child to read the short, simple text at the top of each page, and read the longer text at the bottom of the page yourself. Taking turns with reading builds up a child's confidence and provides the additional fun of joining in. It is a great day when children discover that they can read a whole story for themselves.

The Christmas Story provides an enjoyable opportunity for parents and children to share the excitement and satisfaction of learning to read.

Betty Root